Mr. Franks came over and sat on my desk.

"Has Mr. Hartz talked to you lately?" He asked, referring to the music and drama teacher.

"No," I answered. What was Mr. Franks up to?

Mr. Franks nodded. "That's what I thought. Well, I'm sure you know that every year Mr. Hartz has the fifth and sixth grade classes put on a spring play. Do you know what this year's spring play is called?"

I shook my head.

"*Eskimo Antics*," said Mr. Franks. "Mr. Hartz is going bananas over it."

At first I didn't believe what I was hearing. I didn't dare believe it.

"And do you know who he wants as student director?" Mr. Franks asked.

I couldn't talk, so I shook my head like a jerk again.

"You're sitting at his desk." And with a big smile, Mr. Franks shook my hand.

Fifth Grade Flop

*Megan Stine and
H. William Stine*

Cover by Susan Tang
Illustrated by Paul Henry

Troll Associates

Fifth Grade Flop

Chapter 1

Seven o'clock—only one hour to go till one of the great moments in my life. How could I possibly wait for one more hour?

I had been waiting for weeks—me and about a hundred million other kids. But now it was only sixty minutes and counting to the world premiere of Matt Springer's brand-new rock-music video. Matt Springer was so hot they were making his new video a prime-time TV special.

I know this probably won't come as a shock to anyone, but I'm a big fan of Matt Springer. Who isn't? And it's not just because he's a rock 'n' roll superstar. Or because he's got so much money he actually tried to buy an island in the state of Hawaii.

I, Andrew Kyle Abel, am the world's most loyal Matt Springer fan because, even though he's so rich and so famous, the only thing he really cares about is writing songs. And I guess that's my story, too.

"Hey, Andrew," my father said, walking into the family room and giving me a friendly poke in the back. "What do you say? You and I'll go to the football game tonight at the high school."

I gulped. And my heart did a quick dive off the high board into a swimming pool with no water. Why? Because when my dad says, "What do you say?" he doesn't really want me to say anything. That's his way of telling me I'm going to do something—like it or not. And I didn't like it.

"Thanks but no thanks, Dad," I answered.

My father cleared his throat, long enough for me to get ready, but not long enough for me to get away.

"What kind of a kid says no to his father about a Friday-night football game?" my father asked. He sounded like a lawyer pleading to a jury—which is exactly what he is and exactly what he does for a living.

But I knew what was really on my dad's mind. He wanted me to go to the game so I could watch my older brother, Rich. He's the quarterback—okay, the *star* quarterback—of the high school football team. And my dad keeps hoping that by watching Rich I'll magically turn into a super athlete.

That wouldn't only just be magical—it would be a miracle. See, I'm not exactly what you'd call athletic. In fact, kids are still talking about what I did when I was in the third grade, and that was two years ago!

I was coming out of the school building for P.E. class, and I tripped over a hockey stick and fell on my face. That was when I realized sports equipment hates me.

"Dad, no way can I go to the game with you."

"Why not?"

"Because of Matt Springer."

My father made an instant decision. "Okay, he can come, too."

"Dad, Matt Springer's not a friend of mine. He's a rock singer, and tonight is the world premiere of his new music video."

My dad nodded. He understood all the words, but he didn't know what I was talking about. "Tape it. Watch it later."

"Watch it later? After everyone in the United States and probably the world has already seen it? Are you kidding?"

"Get your shoes on," my dad answered.

His voice convinced me he wasn't kidding.

"I don't believe this," I grumbled at my dad. "How would *you* like to miss one of the great moments in your life because of a football game?"

"How do you know this football game won't be one of the great moments of your life?" my father asked. I hate it when he answers my question with a question.

"Because there are three places you never have a great moment: a principal's office, a dentist's office, and a football game."

This time he didn't think about it even for a second. "Get your coat," he told me. "It's cold out."

So I went down the hallway to the front door and took my down vest off the hook on the wall. As I was putting it on, the doorbell rang. I opened it, knowing it would be my best friend, Robbie Zarkowski. We were supposed to watch the Springer video together at my house.

"Brrr," Robbie said.

He's a really thin kid, so even though it was only September he was already wearing a down parka with his matching knit scarf and a cap that said ROBBIE on it.

Robbie and I have been best friends for so

long that he can almost read my mind. But this time he didn't have to. He just looked at my face then at my coat.

"Let me guess: your dad is forcing you to go to another football game and you'll miss the Springer video," Robbie said, shaking his head.

"It's going to be one of the great moments in my life. My dad guarantees it," I sighed.

Robbie came along to the game with me and missed the Springer video, too. He's that kind of friend. But as we walked over to the high school stadium, he started to worry.

"What'll we do if we're at the game and we run into someone who's seen the Springer video and they start to tell us all about it?" Robbie loves long questions.

"We won't have any choice," I said grumpily. "We'll have to strangle them."

"I don't think missing a rock 'n' roll video is an acceptable defense for a murder charge," my dad said.

Maybe he had a point, but I wasn't really in the mood to hear it.

At the stadium, my dad and Robbie and I climbed halfway up the cold, wooden bleachers until we got to row 17. Dad always sat in the same row as the number on Rich's uniform. As we shuffled in front of a bunch of other serious football parents who were waving green and gold flags, I tripped over someone's foot and almost fell over into row 16. My dad glared at me, like he thought I had done it on purpose. What did he think? Falling down was my favorite hobby? Finally we sat down in the middle of the row and the game started.

Every time Rich threw the ball, my dad jumped to his feet and started shouting. "Did you see that pass? Did you see that pass!"

"Saw it, Dad," I said.

And every time Rich ran with the ball, my Dad shouted, "Look at that run!"

"Looking, Dad," I said.

Rich couldn't do anything wrong on the football field—or anywhere else—as far as my dad was concerned. To my dad, if you were good at sports, you were good at everything. Period.

Now I know what you're thinking. You're thinking that the whole time I was sitting there, freezing and missing the Matt Springer rock video, I was hoping Rich would get tackled so hard they'd have to carry him out on a stretcher. But you're 100 percent wrong.

Rich really is a great older brother. He never plays superjock with me. And he doesn't tell me to get lost when his high school friends come over. I figure Rich must know what a pain it is, my always being compared to him. So he goes out of his way to be nice. And he really likes the funny songs I write.

Anyway, the game went on ... and on. Rich kept passing and running and racking up the points for the Greatdale High School Rockets. You could have heard me cheering for him, too, if my dad hadn't been cheering so much louder.

At halftime the high school marching band started playing the fight song. The minute it started, everyone on our side of the stadium jumped up as if the bleachers had bitten them. They all sang along with the band:

> *"Fight on, you Rockets. Let's give a cheer!*
> *Tell our opponents Greatdale is here.*
> *Wave the green and gold on high*
> *Vic-tor-y is our cry!"*

Once everyone got that out of their systems, Robbie and I started singing the version of the fight song that *I* wrote.

> *"Wake up, you Rockets. Give us a break.*
> *How many nerds do you think we can take?*
> *Wave the white flag. Don't even try.*
> *Give up now is our cry!"*

15

My dad looked at me as if I were Benedict Arnold, but some high school kids who were sitting a couple rows behind us started shouting "Hey, you!"

There were five of them, all wearing the same kind of black leather jacket. It said TRANSFUSION in drippy blood-red letters. Transfusion was the name of the coolest garage band in town. "Sing it again!" they called.

Robbie and I looked at each other. We were both a little surprised, but I didn't have to be asked twice. This time, a few more kids around us laughed, even though *all* the parents scowled. Then Transfusion started singing my song, in a punk sort of way. Pretty soon it spread like a wave around the stadium.

After the game, Robbie and I couldn't wait to get back home and see the Springer video on tape. But my dad killed that idea in ten words or less.

"Let's go to Dixon's. What do you say?" he said.

Dixon's is the burger and ice cream place my dad always went to with Rich after little league games or peewee soccer games and stuff like that. Of course, now that Rich is in high school he wouldn't be caught dead going out with my dad. About the only time he's *ever* seen in the same place with my parents is at the dinner table.

"Order something small," I mumbled to Robbie when we sat down at a corner booth. "That way we'll get out of here fast so we can see the Springer video sooner."

Robbie nodded and when the waiter came, he ordered half a scoop of pistachio ice cream. I ordered the other half.

"Half a scoop?" my father said. "Hey, guys, this is a celebration. Greatdale is on its way to the play-offs. We won big." He smiled at the waiter. "Bring us a Monster."

"A Monster?!" the waiter yelled.

As soon as he did, someone behind the ice cream counter started ringing a bell and everyone in the place stamped their feet and banged their spoons on their tables. It was a lot of noise—but the Monster was a lot of ice cream. Ten scoops, five syrups, and probably half a can of whipped cream. I couldn't believe it because my dad and I had never had one before.

When the Monster came, it looked like a trophy you'd get after winning the World Series. It was in a big glass bowl that seemed to take up the whole table.

"I'm going to be cold for a month," Robbie said, zipping up his jacket before lifting his spoon.

My dad smiled and started to dig in. "I remember the first time Rich and I had one of these babies," he said, scraping away layers of whipped cream to get to the hot fudge. "It was right after he pitched his first perfect no-hitter."

For some reason, I wasn't too hungry. Then I heard someone call my name.

"Hey, Andrew!"

I looked up and saw Wesley Waxner running to our table. I thought he was coming over just to look at the Monster, so I picked up my spoon again.

"Did you see the new Springer video?" Wesley asked.

"Not yet," I said.

"You got to be kidding!" Wesley said.

I tried to add "don't say anything about it" as loud and fast as I could.

But Wesley was faster. "He comes on stage in a penguin costume! And he's got a fish-shape guitar. It's totally fabulous. I can't believe you guys missed it."

Missed it? I never wanted to see it as long as I lived!

Chapter 2

So it was a bad fall season. But I got over being mad about missing the Springer video pretty fast. It took only three weeks.

I snapped out of it when some cool things started happening at school, mostly because of my teacher, Mr. Franks. He is the best teacher at Southside Elementary because he always does things differently. I mean, like the first week of school, when we were studying the Pilgrims landing in America, he wouldn't speak a word of English. He pretended he was a Native American and we had to find some new way to communicate with him.

And then last week, when we started studying the Revolutionary War, he told half the class to wear all red clothes, and the other half to wear brown. But he wouldn't tell us why.

The next morning, I was almost late to school because I couldn't find my brown shirt. So I had to run for Mr. Franks' classroom to make it before the final bell rang. And there was something slippery on the floor. I don't want to say it was a banana peel because that's too stupid to be true . . . but honestly it *did* look like banana slime. Like someone had dropped a piece of banana and then stepped on it, squish.

Anyway I went sliding and suddenly *crash!* I was flying down the hall, doing an imitation of a jet coming in for a landing. I smacked my elbow hard on the floor on the way down.

"Who taught you that move? Your brother?" Michael Thurman asked with a laugh. Michael is a muscle that learned to talk. Just because he thinks he's a superjock, he's always riding me about Rich.

I've known him since kindergarten when he used to tease me all the time about being a klutz. Okay, everyone did that when we were five years old—calling each other names and stuff. But Thurman is still doing it.

"What's that slimy stuff I slipped on, Thurman? Your brain?" I said. Oh brother, now he's got *me* calling names.

I walked into Mr. Franks' classroom, holding my elbow. Michael followed me, still laughing.

"Okay, you guys," Mr. Franks announced, "we're not just going to study the Revolutionary War today. We're going to fight it. I want everyone wearing red to grab a chalkboard eraser—I borrowed extra ones from some of the other classrooms—and form a straight line in front of the class. You guys are the British redcoats."

Half the class got up, including Robbie and Michael Thurman.

"I want everyone in brown to grab an eraser, too," Mr. Franks said. "You guys are the minutemen. Hide behind your chairs and desks and throw erasers at the redcoats."

Well, the erasers started flying everywhere. What a battle! It felt especially great to blast Michael Thurman. Pretty soon his red shirt was covered with chalk dust. But none of the minutemen were getting hit.

"Hey, no fair," Michael said. "They can just bomb us, but we can't hit them because they're hiding."

"Right, Michael," said Mr. Franks. He was sitting on his desk wearing a red shirt and brown pants. "That's the way it was in the real Revolutionary War. No one had ever thought of hiding and taking cover during battle, because they thought it was cowardly."

"Cowardly?" Robbie said with a laugh. "It's the only way to stay alive during a war!"

"I know," Mr. Franks said. "But the American minutemen were the first ones to do it. So even though the minutemen were outnumbered by the redcoats, they won. Maybe you'll want to talk more about this during your oral reports."

"What oral reports?" someone asked.

"Good question," Mr. Franks answered. "I want you all to do oral reports as part of our study of the Revolutionary War."

Everyone started talking at once, asking all the usual questions. Do we have to do it? How long does it have to be? Do we really have to do it? Do we have to memorize it? Can we use notes?

But I had an idea for my report, and I asked, "Can we use electronic equipment?"

"Surprise me, Andrew," Mr. Franks said with a smile.

Now, here's what I want to know: how can there be a teacher like Mr. Franks and a teacher like Mr. Boggs in the same school? Or, forget school—how about in the same universe?

Mr. Boggs is our P.E. teacher, and I guess he was a pretty serious athlete about thirty pounds ago. But now he thinks blowing a whistle and yelling qualifies as teaching P.E. And his favorite person to yell at is—you guessed it—me.

The same day Mr. Franks assigned our oral reports, Mr. Boggs announced a special event of his own.

"Okay, class, listen up!" Mr. Boggs shouted between blasts of the silver whistle he always wore around his neck. "Quiet down."

"We're not talking. That's our teeth chattering," I said. Hey, this was November and the whole class was standing outside in shorts and T-shirts. Give me a break.

Mr. Boggs glared at us. "At the end of school this year," he said, "Southside Elementary will hold its own mini-Olympics competition. Do you know what this means?"

"Yeah, it means that I'm going to have to be sick and stay home one day at the end of school," I told Robbie.

"Each and every one of you will choose a sport, a summer Olympic sport," Mr. Boggs continued, "and for the rest of the year, you're going to train hard so you can compete at your best. Does everyone understand?"

Hey, even a sofa would get the message. "It means you're going to work us to death." I thought I said it quietly, but Mr. Boggs heard it and suddenly was staring at me real hard.

"Are you sure you and Rich Abel are really brothers?" Mr. Boggs asked.

Here we go again.

"See me after school, Andrew. We need to have a conference."

We didn't really need to have a conference. "Boggsy" and I had already had five of them, even though the school year was only two months old.

As I slowly ran around the track during P.E., I thought about the mini-Olympics. The idea of competing in front of everyone at Southside was pretty scary. I'd never fallen down in front of so many people before.

"What are you going to choose?" Robbie asked as he caught up to me on the track.

"Are you kidding? I won't have to choose. Mr. Boggs will forget about me and concentrate on the kids who can win."

Robbie shook his head like he thought I was kidding myself.

After school I went back to Mr. Boggs's office, which was just off the gym. He had it filled with posters of famous athletes and photos and trophies. There was even a newspaper picture of Rich on the bulletin board.

"Andrew, what am I going to do with you?" he asked.

"I was thinking I'd like to be principal," I said. "Think you could help?"

He sighed, which just shows you what's wrong with Boggsy. Mr. Franks would've at least laughed.

"The first week of school, you dropped a bat on your foot," Mr. Boggs began, his feet on his desk.

"Those metal bats are surprisingly slippery," I tried to explain.

"Andrew," the gym teacher sighed, "it was only a twenty-ouncer, but you limped around and missed two gym classes. After that, you got hit in the eye with a football and had a black eye for two weeks."

"Freak accident, for sure," I said.

"I'll say it was a freak accident," Mr. Boggs said, swinging his feet to the floor. "Nobody threw the ball at you. You were carrying it!"

"I'm pretty unlucky that way," I said.

"Andrew, I'm on to you and your tricks. In my book, you're nothing but a faker. But before the year is out, you're going to learn one thing. When you're in my class, you give two hundred percent, or you're going to regret it."

I nodded because he was right—I regretted being in his class already. But I wasn't going to fight with him. I just wanted out of there. When I reached for the doorknob to leave, I stubbed my thumb.

I left school thinking about what Mr. Boggs

had said. I'm *not* a faker. And I know I'm not the first kid in his class who couldn't hit a fastball or throw a baseball so it went forward. Boggsy was making the same mistake as my father: just because my name was Abel and Rich's name was Abel, who said we should be *able* to do the same things.

Luckily, I was on my way to Betty Miller's house, so I stopped worrying about the whole thing.

I should explain. Betty Miller is my piano teacher and has been since I was five. And walking into her house is like walking into a different world. I start playing and I forget all the clumsy things I've done in my life, like missing my mouth with a full glass of milk, or going around all day with my shirt buttoned wrong. When I'm at the piano, I'm never a klutz. I can pretty much play whatever I want to play, whatever I hear in my head.

"Tell me about your day," Betty Miller said, sitting at the grand piano in her huge living room. She always tilts her head to the side and gives me this huge smile that tells me I'm one of her favorite students.

"Well," I began.

"Not in words," she said, shaking her curly black hair. She's really young and pretty, and doesn't look anything like the piano teachers that other kids have. She pointed at the keyboard, still smiling. "Tell me musically."

So I started playing and at first the music was fast and happy until I broke in with a loud crash of chords when I thought about Mr. Boggs. Then the music got soft and mysterious—that was our math quiz I forgot to study for—and weird—that was the seafood stew in the cafeteria. Finally the music got happy again because I thought about coming to my music lesson.

"That was wonderful, Andrew," Betty said, applauding when I finished. "How would you like to do some improvising like that at our next recital? I think everyone would enjoy it."

I immediately thought of one person who probably wouldn't like it.

"Do you think your father will be able to come to the next recital?" she asked.

Was she reading my mind?

"My dad? Come to hear me play piano? What a joke," I said. "The happiest day of my father's life was the day I told him I had perfect pitch."

Betty smiled. "I'll bet he was really proud," she said.

"For about thirty seconds," I said. "He thought I meant I pitched a perfect no-hitter baseball game. When I told him it meant I

could name any note on the piano just by hearing it, he wasn't too impressed."

"Andrew," Betty said, still cheerful, "people can always change their minds."

"Yeah," I agreed glumly. "But with my dad, getting him to change his mind would probably take serious surgery!"

Still, maybe she was right. Maybe I *could* get him to come to my recital. And maybe—if he actually listened to my playing and heard everyone clapping at the end—maybe *then* he'd get the idea that there is something I can do right.

Chapter 3

We did our oral reports on the Revolutionary War right before Christmas vacation. Everyone had maps and drawings and charts on their desks. But all I had on my desk was a tape recorder. I was really nervous. Was anyone going to like my report? Was anyone going to get it?

I had to give my report first. That's what happens when you have a name like Andrew Abel. I carried my tape recorder to the front of the room and put it on Mr. Franks' desk. I knew everyone was wondering what I was going to do next, so I cleared my throat—just to make them think I was going to start talking. But I didn't say a word. Instead, I hit the

PLAY button, walked back to my desk, and sat down.

A few seconds later the music started blasting —loud rock music. That was my report. I had edited together different parts of a lot of songs and made a story out of them. The music was supposed to tell how the patriots felt about independence and how they fought for it.

For instance, I took part of a Matt Springer song where he sings "way to go" over and over again. That was Paul Revere on his ride. Then I edited in a song with Tom Frantic singing "but I'm going to make it."

I also took words from a lot of other songs: "they're coming," "it's war," "go back where you came from," "I want my freedom." The whole thing ended five minutes later with a big explosion and a cool rock version of Yankee Doodle.

When it was over, Mr. Franks asked for comments and a lot of hands went up.

Usually this is a drag because people just say lame things like, "It was a very nice report," or "I thought you did a good job of reading." But it wasn't like that this time. I could tell, just by the way people raised their hands, they had things they really wanted to say.

"Where's his report?" Michael Thurman asked. He sounded almost angry.

I should have known Thurman wouldn't get it. Just because I didn't spend three weeks writing doesn't mean I didn't spend three weeks working on it.

A couple of kids said they agreed with Michael: a tape wasn't a report. But a bunch of kids said they liked it. Finally, Mr. Franks gave his comments.

"Andrew, your report was very different and original," he said. "More important, I think it shows a strong understanding of the sequence of events that led up to the Revolutionary War. I think you understand, too, the emotions and passions that people felt. It's a winner. You should be proud."

Proud? That wasn't a big enough word for how I felt. I knew I was taking a chance, and it had paid off.

A few days later, Mr. Franks played it for one of the other teachers, who told me she loved it. Even some sixth-graders came up to me and said they heard my report. Hey—is this how it feels to be a star?

I was feeling so great that week that I even walked into P.E. class smiling. I should have known that was a mistake.

"Andrew." Mr. Boggs pulled me aside while

the other kids were warming up and shooting some baskets. "It's been four weeks and you still haven't named your sport for the school mini-Olympics."

"Don't worry. I've already picked one," I said quickly. "The hundred-meter dash."

I don't know where that idea came from, I just blurted it out. It seemed like a good idea at the time. Until I talked to Robbie.

"The hundred-meter dash?" he said, staring at me. "You've got to be kidding. You have to run superfast in that race."

It was the last day before Christmas vacation. We were in the library, looking through sports magazines.

"But it's perfect," I explained, pointing to a picture of a sprinter. "See? There's no equipment, so that takes care of me dropping something on my foot or tripping and getting smacked in the head. And it's a short race, so it'll be over fast. And best of all, it's running. Everyone knows how to run, so there's nothing to learn."

"Wrong," Robbie said. "There's a lot of stuff you've got to know about. What about your starting position?"

"Starting position?"

"Yeah. How are you going to start the race?" Robbie said.

"Easy. I'll fire the gun," I said with a grin.

"Pathetic." Robbie shook his head.

"But that's the beauty of the hundred-meter dash," I argued. "I don't have to train or do anything to come in last. I'm already a natural for it."

"Yeah, but maybe if you did train, you wouldn't have to come in last," Robbie said.

What was *he* so upset about? Mr. Boggs wasn't mad when I told him what sport I'd chosen. All he said was, "Oh, brother, you've got your work cut out for you." He *would* bring up my brother!

Luckily, Christmas vacation would give me a two-week break from thinking about the mini-Olympics.

My vacation got off to a really great start. Robbie called early the first morning to tell me four words all Southside kids wait to hear: "The lake froze over."

Now I admit, most kids wait for the lake to freeze so they can go skating. But not me. I go to the lake to watch everyone else skate.

It's a stupid little lake right in the middle of town. Other lakes get cool names like Lake Superior and Lake Hope. This one's called Lake Brad because fifty years ago old Mr. Brad, the richest man in town, had it created and then named if after himself.

I've written some funny songs about the lake and Mr. Brad. My favorite is called "Go Jump in Your Lake, Mr. Brad." Every time the lake freezes over, I write a new verse.

As soon as I got to the lake, Robbie wanted to hear the latest verse. So I sang:

"Let's talk turkey, Mr. Brad.
Because you're the biggest one we ever had.
You built your lake and that's not a sin.
Now do us all a favor, and please jump in."

After that, some kids like Andy Lynch and Ted Ely wanted to hear more. They wanted to hear all the verses I'd written for the song. I was getting big laughs until my audience started getting cold. Then they all went skating again.

The next afternoon we were all at the lake again. At about 4:30 I saw a car stop by the park. It was my dad coming home early. He honked and waved, so I ran over. Great time to talk to him about my Christmas list, I thought. I'd been trying to catch him alone like this for about five days.

"Hi, Dad," I said, hopping into the car.

"Hi," he said, smiling. "You look frozen."

"Yeah, we're having a great time," I said.

"Boy, I loved skating when I was a kid. You

know, the first time I put skates on, I just took off. I was a natural."

"I wasn't really skating," I admitted. "No skates, remember? But I wrote a new verse to my Mr. Brad song. Want to hear it?"

"Hmmm," my dad said, pulling up to a red light. I can never tell if he's listening when my dad says "hmm."

"Well, later, I guess," I said. "Hey, Dad, do you think I'm going to get a synthesizer for Christmas?"

"Can't tell you," my dad said. "All parents have to sign a legal agreement not to reveal any Christmas presents before Christmas day." I knew he was enjoying teasing me. But I think he knew how much I wanted the keyboard, too.

Christmas morning in the living room, all of us were around the tree. The decorations were almost blinding because my mom's into heavy lights and tinsel. As a joke, Rich and I wore sunglasses. My mom thought it was pretty funny.

We opened our presents really fast. Rich gave me some cool tapes and Mom gave me a real camera—one you can actually focus. It was totally great.

Then my dad gave me his present. I couldn't believe it when I unwrapped the box. Inside was a brand-new shiny pair of *hockey skates*!

"Skates?!" I said practically shouting. But it

was the only way I could drown out my pounding heart. "Why'd you give me *skates*?"

"Because I thought you wanted them," my father said. I could tell he was trying not to look angry, but he kept twisting the belt of his bathrobe.

"Perfect. Last year when I asked for an electric guitar, you gave me a catcher's mitt. The year before I asked for a drum machine, but you gave me a tennis racquet. If I ask for a trumpet, what'll you give me? Braces for my teeth?"

"Andrew, it's Christmas—" my mother said, but my dad cut her off.

"Look," he said. He wasn't so calm now. "I saw you standing there all by yourself at the lake, day after day, while everyone else was skating. What did you expect me to think? I figured you felt left out. You need to be active like other kids instead of playing the piano indoors for hours."

I wanted to explain to my dad that if he just would stop telling me what I need, maybe for once he'd see what I want. Instead, I ran out of the living room and took the stairs two at a time.

I slammed the door to my room and sat on my bed with no lights on. Only 365 more shopping days until my next disappointment.

Chapter 4

*T*hings were pretty quiet around my house after Christmas. It got especially quiet every time my dad and I were in the same room.

One night I heard him talking to my mom when they didn't know I was listening. "I don't know what I did wrong," he said.

If my dad thought *he* did something wrong, why was he acting like everything was my fault? I didn't get it. You probably guessed—I was pretty glad when school started again.

"Happy New Year and welcome back, gang," Mr. Franks told us. "Who got something interesting for Christmas? Raise your hands. Something *interesting*: a new first name? Anybody? New ears? A third arm?"

The class giggled. What else can you do when a grown-up acts like a total goof? It felt like the first time in months I had actually laughed.

"Sounds like a boring Christmas, gang," Mr. Franks said, shaking his head. He started walking up and down the aisles. "Okay, let me ask you a different question. If you built a house out of ice, would it keep you warm?" He asked another question before we could answer. "If the sun never set, how would you know when it's day or night? Or when to go to bed?"

"What's the answer?" Jackie Clipper asked. He can't take being kept in suspense for more than ten seconds.

"We're not going to find out today, Jackie," said Mr. Franks. "But for the next month we're going to learn about some interesting people—the Eskimos."

Mr. Franks turned off the lights and turned on a slide projector. He went on talking, walking around the class at the same time. "It's still a mystery where the Eskimos came from," he explained, "but we know they've lived in the same places for more than a thousand years."

Mr. Franks stopped next to Gary Tischler's desk. "What's the first thing you want to know about the Eskimos? Quickly. First thing out of your head."

Gary thought for just a second and blurted out, "Uh—do they speak English?"

"Some have learned English, but Eskimos also have their own languages. Then he turned and pointed at me. "Abel—what do *you* want to know?"

I didn't have time to think, just talk. "What kind of laws do they have?" I asked.

"Spoken like a lawyer's son. Your father would be proud of you," Mr. Franks said, smiling.

Yeah. I'll believe that when I see it.

"Well, Andrew, they have no *written* laws, but they also have no police or lawyers or courts. They don't need them. We'll learn more about that in the weeks to come. Now I have a question for all of you: what do they use for windows in their igloos? See if you can find out by tomorrow. Right now it's time to move on to math."

That's how we started studying Eskimos. When Mr. Franks starts a subject he really gets into it. That must be why we do, too. Sometimes we had spelling tests about Eskimos, or we studied the maps of where they live. In science we even studied how to build an igloo and how they actually keep you warm.

Every day Mr. Franks set aside fifteen minutes in the morning and fifteen minutes in the afternoon as Think Times. We were supposed to be thinking about a written research project. Remembering the success of my Revolutionary War report, I decided to write a musical comedy about Eskimos.

I got to work on it right away. First, I came up with a title: *Eskimo Antics*. I was writing all the dialogue and the music and lyrics, but every time I even looked at the piano, my dad would think of some way to get me away from it. Chores around the house. Thank-you notes to relatives for Christmas gifts. Friday nights were the absolute worst.

"Hey, how about you and me going to the basketball game tonight? What do you say?"

My dad said the same thing every Friday night. Half an hour later I'd be killing my back sitting on the narrow wooden bleachers in the smelly high school gym. That was the bad part.

The good part was watching Rich play basketball. He shot one-point baskets. He shot two-point baskets. He shot three-point baskets. If there was such a thing as a shot from the locker room for five points, Rich could have done it. He was amazing.

Usually I didn't tell Dad what I thought

about Rich because he was too busy telling me what *he* thought about Rich to listen to me.

But one week, while my dad talked on and on, I planned what to say. Why do you drag me to these games? I wanted to tell him I wasn't going to these stupid games anymore.

Just as I was about to open my mouth, my dad did the strangest thing. There was a time-out on the court and the crowd was kind of quiet, even though the cheerleaders were yelling their lungs out. My dad wasn't looking at me, but he put his arm around my shoulder. He kept it there until the buzzer rang and the time-out was over. Then everyone stood up while the band played the fight song.

Why did he do that? And then why did he act like he didn't do it? I was so confused.

"If we win, we'll go to Dixon's," my dad said. "What do you say?"

I nodded. Sure, why not? Maybe we could talk. Maybe I'd tell him about *Eskimo Antics*.

I looked around at the crowd. There was a high school guy and his girlfriend sitting a couple of rows away. They weren't watching the game. They both had headphones plugged into a portable tape player and were listening to music. Hey, that's the way to enjoy a basketball game, I thought to myself.

My dad nudged me. He was looking at the

two high school kids, too. "Do you believe Bozo and Bozette over there?" he asked. "They'd rather listen to music and miss the game? Give me a break." He shook his head.

Right then I knew I wasn't going to have a good time at Dixon's that night.

All through January, my dad didn't miss a single home basketball game . . . and, unfortunately, neither did I. And February wasn't looking any better, except that I turned in my play, *Eskimo Antics*. Boy, did I work hard on it. After that, there wasn't much going on for me in school.

I guess that's what you call the lull before the storm. The storm hit early in February.

"I want to see you during recess," Mr. Franks said before class started.

I froze. Mr. Franks only saw kids during recess to shout at them because he was too nice a guy to do it in front of the whole class.

Now I'm not saying I didn't give him some reasons to be mad at me. Recently I'd been what teachers like to call "out of control" in class. Talking out a lot, not doing such a good job on my homework. But it was only because I had been so excited about writing my Eskimo play.

The class emptied out fast at recess, and Mr. Franks took his time coming over to sit on my desk. "Has Mr. Hartz talked to you lately?" he asked, referring to the music and drama teacher.

"No," I answered. What was Mr. Franks up to?

Mr. Franks nodded. "That's what I thought. Well, I'm sure you know that every year Mr. Hartz has the fifth and sixth grade classes put on a spring play. Do you know what this year's spring play is called?"

I shook my head.

"*Eskimo Antics*," said Mr. Franks. "Mr. Hartz is going bananas over it."

At first I didn't believe what I was hearing. I didn't dare believe it.

"And do you know who he wants as student director?" Mr. Franks asked.

I couldn't talk, so I shook my head like a jerk again.

"You're sitting at his desk." And with a big smile, Mr. Franks shook my hand.

Chapter 5

You don't have to be with our music and drama teacher very long to know that you've never known anyone like him before. Mr. Hartz is tall and very thin and wears his blond hair kind of long in back.

The great thing about him is that he gets totally excited about everything. When he teaches us new songs, he sings them to us. If it's a sad song, he actually almost gets tears in his eyes. Lots of kids think he's a total jerk, but lots of kids like him because he's basically a positive, happy kind of guy. I'm in between.

Still, I walked into the music room after school really excited about *Eskimo Antics* being the spring play.

"Sit down, Andrew!" Mr. Hartz said. He was sitting on a stack of newspapers he collected for recycling.

I sat down at the end of the semicircle of wooden chairs.

"No, there," Mr. Hartz said, pointing slowly to the piano. "I want to hear the songs you wrote for your play," he explained.

I walked over to the piano and played my four songs, "Iceberg Rock," "Give Him the Cold Shoulder," "Big Lou Igloo," and "Blubber Blues." Mr. Hartz laughed at the jokes the whole time I was singing. When I finished, he applauded like crazy. Talk about a good audience.

"Okay. Let's talk about your play," he said, pulling a chair up until he was about a foot from me. "It's brilliant!"

"Thanks," I said, grinning like an idiot. And for the next twenty minutes, all we did was talk about *me* and how great the spring play was going to be because of *me*! It was almost too good to be true. I half expected a bucket of bricks to fall on my head when I walked outside.

By the first week in March, Mr. Hartz said we were ready to hold auditions for actors. We put up signs all over school. That Friday I got to sit in the audience next to

Mr. Hartz and watch all the kids trying out on stage.

There are six main characters in *Eskimo Antics*. First there's Tuvat, who's a kid about my age. Then there's his mother and his father, his older brother, Rejev, and Big Lou Igloo, a wise old man. Finally, there's the seal, who has a really important part in the play. He has to follow Tuvat around the whole time because that's the story. It's about how this seal sort of attaches itself to Tuvat, who can't get rid of him.

There are plenty of other Eskimos in the play, but Tuvat is the most important. He sings two of the songs and has most of the jokes. Whoever played Tuvat had to be really funny and know the best ways to tell jokes.

We sat and watched as about twenty kids from the fifth and sixth grades performed one by one. Some of them were definite thumbs-down. Harry Beech had a loud voice, but he couldn't carry a tune in a plastic bag.

"Sorry," Mr. Hartz said, when Harry's song was over.

Marjorie Benham didn't sing at all. She twirled a baton—for about ten seconds.

"Sorry," called Mr. Hartz. "Eskimos don't have baton twirlers."

Marjorie was out. I wondered when Mr.

Hartz was going to start asking me what I thought. After all, I was the author and I was supposed to be the student director, too!

Sara Smith-Brown walked to the front of the stage. She was shivering with her arms folded across her chest.

"Good shivering," Mr. Hartz shouted. "Great acting."

"Who's acting?" Sara said. "This auditorium is freezing."

"Sara, you'll play Tuvat's mother," Mr. Hartz said without even looking at me. He decided just as quickly that Josh Baldwin would play Tuvat's father and Ben Ku would play Rejev, Tuvat's older brother. Then he picked little Mickey Morgan to be the seal.

Michael Thurman came out next. "What do you want me to do?" he asked from center stage.

I wanted him to fall through a hole in the floor.

But Mr. Hartz didn't agree. "I know your singing from class," Mr. Hartz said. "And I've heard you tell a joke or two. You'll be perfect for Big Lou Igloo."

"Michael Thurman?" I said to Mr. Hartz, jumping to my feet.

How could Mr. Hartz do this? Michael Thurman in my play? I didn't want that tube-head to even come to the play. I dropped back down on my seat like a rock. Unbelievable.

"Trust me, Andrew. And now, we have to decide who will play Tuvat," Mr. Hartz announced as he looked at the group on the stage. "Iggy, would you sing a song for us?"

Sure. It figured. He was going to give Iggy Parker, his favorite sixth-grader, the part of Tuvat. Iggy Parker is this skinny kid with wavy black hair and crooked glasses. He is so totally Mr. Hartz's pet student, he practically comes to school wearing a leash!

Iggy sang "America" and Mr. Hartz stood up and applauded at the end. "What a beautiful and resonant singing voice, Iggy," the teacher gushed. "Let's hear you tell a joke."

Iggy's mouth moved, but Mr. Hartz and I couldn't hear what he said.

"Speak up, Iggy," Mr. Hartz ordered. "I can't hear you."

Again we saw Iggy's mouth move, but we didn't hear him.

Josh Baldwin, who was standing near Iggy, said, "He says to tell you he *is* speaking up, Mr. Hartz."

I almost lost it. "Mr. Hartz, Iggy can't play Tuvat," I said. "He's had stage fright ever since the second grade. No one will hear him."

"Well, what are we going to do?" Mr. Hartz asked. "There's no one else who can play the part."

The truth is, I could think of one person who could really play the part right—me! But I had been too nervous to tell Mr. Hartz that's what I wanted, especially when I knew he wanted Iggy. But now I decided to risk it.

"I can do it," I said.

At first I didn't know whether he was going to laugh or cry. "This isn't a one-man show, Andrew."

"Give me a chance," I said. And before I knew what I was doing, I was on my way up to the stage. My heart was pounding. Someone handed me a script, but of course, I didn't need one. I just started reciting the part from memory.

"Hi," I said. "Welcome to the Yukon. Cold enough for you? Do you know why they call this place the Yukon? Because when the first settlers came here, they checked out the thermometer, saw how cold it was, and said, 'Yukon have it.' They packed up and left the next day.

"My name is Tuvat. That's an Eskimo name. It means 'nose that never stops dripping.' If you think that's bad, you should meet my older brother, Rejev. That means 'teeth that never stop chattering.' Then there's my mother, Barta, 'hands that never stop cooking,' and my dad, Sverq, 'mouth that never stops eating.'

"My problem is I've got this seal that won't stop following me around so I'm looking for the wise man, Big Lou Igloo. I hope he can help me get rid of the seal. Big Lou is also a great Eskimo mathematician. One day he was skating around in circles, and right after that he invented Eskimo Pi. I hope he can solve my problem."

Kids were laughing at all the jokes, and when I stopped talking, Robbie and some of my other friends started clapping real loud. So Mr. Hartz had to give me the part of Tuvat.

The next day was Saturday, and Robbie and I were playing some video games at his house.

"Wow," said Robbie, "I can't believe you're going to star in your own play."

"I wanted it pretty bad," I admitted, shooting down twelve jet-pack wing gorillas.

"But what happens if you memorize the whole play and you rehearse for days and days and you always get all the words right but when all the parents are there you get nervous or something and you forget what you're supposed to say and you don't know what to do?"

Sometimes by the time Robbie gets to the end of a question, I've forgotten the beginning.

"It won't happen," I said. "I totally loved being on the stage. I wasn't nervous or klutzy or anything. I think I must be immune to stage fright."

"Hey, you want to go to the high school track later and practice for the hundred-meter dash?" Robbie asked. "So far, you've practiced once and ran for only about one meter. What about the other ninety-nine?"

"No way. I've got too many things to do for the play to worry about that."

"You're going to have to run sometime."

I turned off the video game and the TV. "Not until months from now."

"You're not scared, are you?" Robbie asked.

For once he asked a short question, and it was like being hit in the stomach. The thing is, I couldn't even tell Robbie what I imagined every time I thought about the race. I saw myself doing something really stupid, like starting before the gun went off or leaning way over the starting line and falling right on my face.

"Andrew, do you know what could happen if you practiced—I mean really practiced?" Robbie said. "You could even win this race."

Win it? What a joke. I knew I was going to come in last by a mile. And, okay, I could live with that. All I really wanted was to finish without falling down.

Chapter 6

All through March, the kids in *Eskimo Antics* were supposed to be learning their parts. Other kids were designing and building sets for the play. Everybody was getting excited about it.

My mom was, too. She kept asking me about the play, but I wouldn't tell her anything because I wanted her to be surprised. Just to be funny, she'd ask me every day, "How many days until opening night?"

When April came, we began to rehearse every day after school and even during music class. Most of the time at the end of a scene, Mr. Hartz would shout from the back of the auditorium, "Brilliant! Perfect." One time he even said he thought we should put mats on the floor because people were going to be rolling in the aisles, laughing.

But once in a while, he'd charge onto the stage, saying, "No, no, no, no, no, *no!*" The man never learned the meaning of *halfway*.

Believe it or not, that made rehearsing even more exciting. Everything was going great until one day when Michael Thurman and I were rehearsing the scene when Tuvat meets Big Lou Igloo.

In the play, Tuvat searches for days and finally finds Big Lou's secret hidden igloo. The scene is supposed to be fast and funny.

"Are you Big Lou Igloo?" I asked.

"I'm not Big Moe Condo," said Michael as Big Lou. "Come in. Sit down on the couch by the warm fire."

"But you don't have a fire," I said.

"That's okay. I don't have a couch, either," Lou said.

"I've been looking for you everywhere."

"I took the day off," Big Lou said. "But since the sun won't set for another six weeks here, the day was longer than I thought."

"Big Lou, I've got a problem for you."

"Well, you can keep it. I've got enough of my own," said Big Lou.

"But," I said, "you're the only man in the village who can help me. My problem is there's a seal that follows me everywhere I go. In fact, he's outside your igloo right now."

"Wonderful. Bring him in and we'll eat him. It's lunchtime and I'm tired of eating cold cuts."

"But that's my problem, Big Lou," I said. "I know that we Eskimos eat seals and make clothes from their skins and melt their blubber for heating oil, but I can't do it. I think the seal wants to be my friend."

Then Big Lou handed me a big piece of blubber and said, "Okay, sit down and let's chew the fat a while."

Then I began to sing my song, "Blubber Blues."

"I've got the Blubber Blues.
I've got the Blubber Blues.
No matter what I choose,
I've got the Blubber Blues.
Don't want to eat the meat. It's no treat.
Don't want to wear the hair. It's no fair.
Don't want to steal a seal. It's no deal.
I'd rather spear a fish. That's my dish.
I've got the Blubber Blues.
I've got the Blubber Blues.
There's no win or lose
with the Blubber Blues."

"Stop, stop, stop, stop, *stop!*" yelled Mr. Hartz. "It's all wrong, all wrong."

All wrong? It sounded great to me. I don't know about everyone else in the auditorium, but I was holding my breath, waiting to hear what Mr. Hartz was going to say next.

He came down to the seats right in front of the stage and motioned with his hands for us to gather around him.

"Last night I had one of the most emotional experiences of my life," he began in a quiet voice. "I was watching TV and do you know what I was watching?" He looked each of us right in our eyes. "It was a program on Eskimos and how they live. And I was deeply moved—I mean, truly deeply touched—by the courage of these brave people who live so simply. They don't have new cars and cable TV and microwave popcorn."

I swear he wiped a tear from his eye.

"Andrew, I want our audience to be moved the way I was moved last night. And that means that 'Blubber Blues' should be just that: the blues. And forget about jokes about couches, because these wonderful people don't have couches. And Big Lou shouldn't be making jokes, either. No one should."

"No jokes?" I said. "If no one makes jokes, no one will laugh."

"Andrew, we can't let the serious—almost tragic—overtones of this play get lost in laughter."

I tried to catch my breath and not lose my temper. "But it's a *comedy*. You said there's nothing more important than making people laugh," I said.

"Except making people cry. Andrew, try it my way," said Mr. Hartz. "Sing the song to Big Lou. And sing it real *slow*—don't sing it as a joke. You'll see. You'll get all choked up. I know you will."

Try it? Was he kidding? Everyone was staring at me, so I sang "Blubber Blues" again while Mr. Hartz played the piano so slowly it sounded like a funeral march. Everyone got very quiet and I even saw Sara Smith-Brown stick her finger in her throat as if she were gagging. I agreed with her. It was totally wrong.

When I was finished, Mr. Hartz said, "There. Doesn't it make you want to cry?"

I stared at him and slowly nodded my head. Yup. I wanted to burst into tears, all right. He was ruining my play!

That night after dinner I stayed in my bedroom with the door closed. I didn't want to see anyone. Mostly I didn't want anyone to ask me how the play was going.

I was lying on my bed, listening to a Matt Springer tape, when Rich came in.

"Hey, jerk," he said.

Lately he had stopped calling me squirt and started calling me jerk. But he always said it with a smile, so I didn't mind.

He got a running start and jumped onto my bed and came down sitting straight up. "Your play's pretty soon, huh?" he said. He shoved me aside so he could take over most of my bed.

"Yeah," I said, laughing and pushing back.

"I can't come, you know."

"Why not?" I asked.

He took my sneaker off the floor and made a set shot with it. It dropped straight into my wastebasket across the room. "Basketball game. Guess where Dad's going to be that night?"

I had to laugh. "Now ask me something hard. I bet you a million dollars I know where Dad's going to be—at your basketball game."

"Pay up, jerk. You just lost a million dollars!" Rich said, sinking my other sneaker into the wastebasket.

"You mean he's coming to my play?"

"For sure," Rich said.

"Oh, no," I moaned and rolled off the bed. I lay on the floor like a dead body.

"What's the matter? I talked him into it,"

Rich said. "He wasn't totally crazy about the idea at first, but I told him he was going to be proud of you. 'Give the little jerk a chance,' I said."

"You said that?"

"Well, I had to lie a little. You're really a *big* jerk." With that Rich grabbed my pillow and pounded me with it for about a whole minute.

After he left, I thought: Thanks a lot, Rich. I know you thought you were doing me a favor, but how could you know that Mr. Hartz was ruining *Eskimo Antics*? Now Dad was coming to see me and my play. And probably after five minutes he'd drag everyone in the audience out of the auditorium and over to the high school gym.

Once I knew my dad was coming to the play, everything changed. I got nervous before every rehearsal—and totally depressed afterward. Mr. Hartz kept telling us to put more emotion into our lines.

I could tell everybody thought it was a bad idea to make *Eskimo Antics* into a serious documentary about Eskimo life. But no one had the nerve to argue with Mr. Hartz. We couldn't have convinced him anyway.

In gym class, even Mr. Boggs noticed how down I was.

"Andrew, you look like you need some good

news. So here it is," he said right before blasting his whistle. It's a miracle he doesn't break windows with that thing. "Class, listen up! I have an announcement about the mini-Olympics."

I crossed my fingers. Please let them be canceled because of extreme cruelty to fifth graders.

No such luck. Boggsy announced that he had decided to group all the fifth-graders into Olympic teams, ten on a team. And each person would get points for his or her event. The winner would get the most points, the loser would get nothing—and everyone else would be somewhere in between. At the end, the team with the most points would win the gold medal in the Olympics.

Way to go Boggsy, I thought. Now, not only was I going to lose the hundred-meter race, but I was going to make my teammates lose points.

For the rest of the class we ran practice races. I came in last every time. Things weren't looking too good.

After P.E., Michael Thurman came up to me. He'd been working really hard on the play every day. I had almost forgotten what a turkey he really was. But he reminded me real fast by pushing me hard into the wall.

"Why don't you run faster?" Michael asked.

"I can't. I wish I could," I said, straightening up. "Don't you ever wish you could do something? Act like a human being, for instance?"

"But you don't even try to run fast. You *never* try."

"What for?" I said. "I might as well try to fly."

Michael pushed me again. "Look, you're on my team. I can't do anything about that. But we'd better not lose the Olympics because you wimped out. I don't think you'd like it if I just didn't try in your play, would you?"

"What's that supposed to mean?"

"You'll see," he said as he walked away.

I found out what Michael meant later that day at the first dress rehearsal. Everything was ready, the costumes, the scenery, the lights, all the actors. But where was Michael Thurman? Where was Big Lou Igloo? We waited a whole hour for Michael, but he never showed up. I couldn't say anything.

Mr. Hartz was furious as he stormed back and forth through the auditorium. Finally, he rolled up his sleeves. "We have work to do. We need someone to stand in for Michael."

Then he said six of the scariest words I'd ever heard.

"Iggy Parker, take Michael's place today!"

Chapter 7

*I*t was eight o'clock at night, and I was sitting all alone in the top row of the high school stadium bleachers. Welcome to "How to Ruin Your Life," I thought to myself. I'm so good at it I should give lessons.

Lesson #1—Have your music and drama teacher change your play from a comedy to a tragedy. If you can't find a teacher as loony as Mr. Hartz, just let me know. I'd be happy to loan him to you.

Lessons #2, #3, and #4—Have Michael Thurman not show up for three—count them, *three*—rehearsals in a row. Which leads right to . . .

Lesson #5—Have your music and drama teacher *permanently* replace Michael Thurman with Iggy Parker, who has stage fright and is about as funny as swimming pool slime.

So in five easy lessons and four short days my life went from unbelievable to unlivable.

I knew I had to do something about it. Michael wasn't going to come through for me because he thought I wasn't even trying to come through for him. And maybe he was right. I tried to say something to him in class one day, but he gave me such a killer look, like "Don't you dare talk to me unless whatever you say is perfect."

I let it slide. I didn't have anything perfect to say. I just wanted him to come to rehearsals. So that's why I was sitting in the bleachers.

"Up here!" I shouted as soon as I saw Robbie come into the stadium.

"Why did you want to meet here instead of coming over to my house or calling me on the phone or sending a telegram or at least meeting somewhere warm?" he asked. His question lasted the entire time he was climbing the stairs to get to me.

"I didn't want anyone to see us," I said. "Listen, you know what a total jock Michael Thurman is. I mean, he's probably got a T-shirt that says 'Sweat Is My Life.' Well, he thinks his team is going to lose the mini-Olympics because of me. Because it looks like I'm not trying to win my race."

"Are you or aren't you?" Robbie asked in a quiet voice.

"Get real. No matter how hard I try, there's no way I can win and I'll probably trip over my own feet."

"So what are you doing *here*?" Robbie asked, shivering even though it was almost fifty degrees outside.

"Well, what I was thinking was maybe I could do better. I mean, if you could sort of show me some things about running."

"The Olympics are only a week away."

"What does that mean? You won't help me? You're giving up on me, too?"

"Of course I'll help you, spud-brain," Robbie said. "It just means we've got to work like crazy. And we'll have to train at night since you have rehearsals every day after school."

We started that night. We went down to the track and Robbie showed me how to get into the starting position. The cold, hard track cinders bit into my hands, and my back hurt from bending over. But we kept at it for two hours.

The next night we got into running.

"Lift your knees! Lift your knees!" Robbie shouted as I ran by. "Push off with each step!"

My legs hurt. My sides ached. My heart pounded. It didn't feel like I was getting any faster, but at least no one could say I wasn't giving it a shot.

Every day after school Michael still didn't show up for rehearsals, but every night until way past dark, Robbie and I practiced at the high school track.

One night I came home pretty late and my dad was already home from work.

"Where've you been?" he asked. He was sitting in the living room reading the paper.

"I've been running around with Robbie."

"Hey, don't you have a race coming up?" he asked.

"Yeah. Couple of days."

He looked like he wanted to ask me more about it. Was I ready for the race? How was I going to do? Was I practicing—that's all it takes, you know, practice.

Come on, Dad, go ahead—ask. For once I really wanted him to, so I could tell him how I'd been training every night. And how even I was starting to believe I might get through the race without falling or some bozo thing like that.

But he didn't ask. He turned the page of the newspaper and changed the subject. "Something else is happening, too, isn't it?" he asked without looking at me.

"You mean my play? It's next week," I said.

"Yeah. Right," he said with a smile. "I'm going to be there. Did you know that?"

"Yeah, Rich told me. Are you sure you don't want to go to Rich's game instead?"

He looked surprised for a second. Then he said, "Listen to me. There's one thing I'm sure about: I want to be there and see your play."

And it's going to be like old times, Dad, I thought as I left the room. You'll watch me fall on my face.

On my way to the kitchen, my mom gave me one of those sympathetic looks, like she understood what I was going through. It made me feel better for about twenty seconds.

Why couldn't it rain on the day of the mini-Olympics? Why did it have to be a beautiful sunny April day? The entire Southside Elementary School marched over to the high school track. The band was playing. Flags were waving on poles. Moms and dads were cheering from the bleachers.

My dad was in court that day, but my mom was there.

"Hi, kiddo," she called to me when I got near the parents' group. I walked over for a minute to talk to her. "Rich said he was going to try to get out of study hall to come see you today," she said, smiling.

"I know. But I told him not to worry. I'll still be running by the time his school gets out."

"Hey, positive attitude, remember? Good luck, Andrew!" my mom said with a big, confident smile.

One by one, kids ran their races and competed in their events. Some of it was even pretty exciting. Gail Rosenblum set a new school record for the standing broad jump. Mickey Morgan did a double back flip in his gymnastics routine.

But I walked around not seeing anything, just getting more and more nervous.

Robbie stayed with me. He'd already won big in two events for his team, and he kept trying to keep me confident.

"You don't have to win. You just have to try," he kept saying.

My race was coming up.

"Hey, Zarkowski, whose team are you on?"

said Harley Fishel, captain of Robbie's team. "Look at the score board."

The score board said that our teams were tied for first, Robbie's and mine. That's why the two captains, Harley Fishel and Michael Thurman, were looking intense enough to eat glass.

"Harley, go bob for apples in the ocean," Robbie said and turned back to me. "Okay, get loose."

He showed me some stretching exercises and we did them together.

"Let's go, Andrew," Mr. Boggs called. "Hundred meter's next."

I looked at Robbie and took a deep breath.

He tried to smile and said, "Keep your knees up. Don't save anything. Give it everything from the gun."

"Runners take your places!" Mr. Boggs shouted.

I got my legs to carry me as far as the starting line. Then I looked down the line of runners—seven of the fastest runners in the fifth grade. They were looking at their feet, getting into their starting positions.

I did the same thing. I shook my arms out one last time, crouched down, and got ready to start. That's when I saw it. My right shoelace was untied! I started to reach for the laces, but just then *bang*! Boggs fired the starting gun!

I took off. We all took off. There was nothing else to do but run like mad and *pray* that my shoe wouldn't come off—and that I wouldn't trip.

I didn't see or hear anything. The only things I knew about in the whole world were my feet and the track.

Knees high, knees high, knees high, I said to myself over and over in rhythm with my running feet.

Right before I got to the finish line I heard the crowd explode with a cheer and I knew the race was over. That meant I hadn't won, but I kept running past the finish line.

"I did it! I finished the race without falling down!" I shouted out loud.

All of a sudden there were arms grabbing me, hugging me, pounding me. Everyone crowded around while I tried to catch my breath. It was Robbie and some kids on my team. Even Rich was there.

"What's wrong with you?" I shouted, trying to push away from them. "Haven't you ever seen a loser before?"

"Spud-brain," Robbie shouted. "You didn't lose. You came in next to last!"

"I did? I didn't lose?" I shouted.

"You were great, you little jerk," Rich said, shaking me by the shoulders.

"You won a point," Michael Thurman said. "I don't believe it, but you won a whole point. Harley Fishel's team member came in last, so they got zip. We're ahead by one point, thanks to you, Andrew."

I turned to Michael and gave him a really angry look. "Hey—I came through for you!" I shouted. "Now stop messing up my play!"

"Okay, okay," Michael said. "Don't get so intense."

There was one more event: the high jump. That was Michael's best event and Harley's, too.

Right before Michael started his jump, he looked over at me and shouted, "Hey, look. It's snooing."

That was a line from my play that Big Lou Igloo said. So I answered him with the next line.

"Snooing? What's snoo?"

"I don't know. What's new with you?" Michael shouted back. And then with a laugh, he took off and jumped the highest he'd ever jumped.

He won the event by a mile and racked up ten points. Harley got only eight. Our team won the mini-Olympics by three points. One of them was mine.

When Mr. Boggs put the gold medal around my neck, I think I actually saw him smile!

Chapter 8

Dear Dad,

I know you're getting home late from your trip to Chicago, but I thought you'd want to see this. It's a gold medal from the school mini-Olympics. Guess what? I don't have to give it back tomorrow. It's mine! Everyone on my team got one. We won the Olympics—do you believe it?—and even I made one point.

Mr. Boggs said we could wear the medal in school tomorrow if we wanted to. But I want you to have it. I don't win them every day and I know you've been waiting for it a long time.

Love,
Andrew

I left it on the table where he always puts his briefcase. In the morning I found a note by my cereal bowl.

Dear Andrew,
  Thanks. I knew you could do it. I'm sure it's only the first of many. I can't wait to see you try it on.

Love,
Dad

I felt kind of good and kind of bad when I read his note. I mean, what am I supposed to do for a dad who's always looking for my *next* victory?

When I got to school, a lot of the kids were still congratulating me.

"Great race, Big A," little Mickey Morgan said.

"Yo, Andrew! Good hustle!" Darlene Robinson said, giving me *two* thumbs-up, which she didn't do very often.

No one seemed to remember that I didn't *win* the race. But, hey, I'm not complaining.

Michael came over to my desk as soon as I sat down.

"We rehearsing today?"

"Mr. Hartz gave your part to Iggy," I said.

"I'll take care of Iggy," Michael said.

Sounded good to me. End of discussion. Meanwhile, I decided I *had* to do something about Mr. Hartz taking all the jokes out of *Eskimo Antics*. I just knew everyone would hate it his way.

So after school on the day of the performance, I took Mr. Hartz aside.

"We have to talk," I told him, and boy did I talk. I went into a long thing about how he had picked me to be the student director, but he hadn't let me direct at all. And now I thought the play was going to be a flop because it wasn't funny.

Then I told him all about my dad and how he was finally coming to see me perform. Mr. Hartz gets pretty emotional about things like that, and I knew it would get to him, which it did.

When I was done, all he said was "You're the author, so do what you want." He even agreed that Michael Thurman could have his part back as Big Lou Igloo—mainly because of the scene where Big Lou is supposed to pick up the seal. Every time Iggy had tried to lift Mickey Morgan, they had both ended up on their backs on the floor.

So that night, before the performance, I called all the cast members together backstage. "Look guys," I said, "We've got to do *Eskimo*

Antics as a comedy—the way we rehearsed it in the beginning. Fast and funny. With the jokes. Okay? Go for the big laughs."

Everyone nodded, but I was more nervous than ever. Would they be able to change back to comedy after rehearsing the play so seriously for the past two weeks? I knew I was really taking a chance. The whole thing might fall apart.

I peeked out through the curtains to get a look at the audience, and my stomach leaped into my throat.

It wasn't like the President of the United States was sitting out there. It was just regular teachers and parents. Just people like my mom and Mr. Franks and Betty Miller . . . and *my dad*.

The lights went down and the curtain went up.

"Break a leg," Mr. Hartz told me.

"You're talking to the right kid," I said, laughing.

"That's theater talk for 'good luck,'" he explained.

I took a deep breath and realized I couldn't remember how to talk. Forget about the lines— I couldn't remember a single word of the play, even though I wrote it! And I thought I was immune to stage fright.

But I didn't have any choice. I had to go on. So I walked out on stage, followed by little Mickey Morgan in his seal costume. The audience applauded as soon as they saw me. And they laughed as soon as they saw the seal. We were off to a good start!

As soon as I opened my mouth to speak, something happened. I remembered what I was supposed to say. I told them my name was Tuvat and that I was an Eskimo in the Yukon and that I was looking for the Eskimo wise man, Big Lou Igloo. Then I explained why I needed his help.

"This seal follows me wherever I go. My parents want me to catch it and kill it so we can have meat and fuel. But I don't want to because I think this seal wants to be my friend. Just six weeks ago at sunset, it was even hiding under my bed."

Then I walked over to the part of the stage where my family's igloo was, and Mickey scooted under the bed.

"Bark, bark!" Mickey said from under my bed.

"What was that?" asked Sara Smith-Brown, who was playing my mother. "It sounded like an animal."

"And it sounded like it came from under your bed, Tuvat," said Josh Baldwin, my father.

I looked under my bed—but only for a split second. "Uh, you're right. There is an animal under my bed," I said. "It's a dust bunny."

"That's no dust bunny," my father said, pulling the seal from under my bed. "It's a nice fat seal. Quick, get the spears, get the nets, and get the lettuce, tomato, and mayonnaise."

The seal gave Josh an enormous loud wet smooch.

"What was that?!" Josh asked, dropping the seal.

"Sealed with a kiss," I said, grinning while Mickey waddled away as fast as he could out of the igloo.

"After him!" Josh shouted.

"Don't worry, Dad. I'll do something about that seal," I said, rushing out of the igloo.

But I wasn't going to look for the seal. Instead, I was going to try to find Big Lou Igloo.

Then Mr. Hartz started playing the piano and I sang the first song, "Big Lou Igloo."

> "Big Lou Igloo, I'm looking for you.
> Big Lou Igloo, I really dig you.
> I'm looking high and low, Lou.
> I'm looking under my snowshoe.
> I'm checking every branch and twig, Lou.
> I'm searching through thin and thig, Lou.
> Big Lou Igloo, where are you?"

The audience loved it, and they kept laughing all the way through the scene when I finally meet Big Lou and sing the "Blubber Blues." Michael was getting great laughs from everyone, too.

After I told Big Lou my problem with the seal, Big Lou said, "Tuvat, if you do not want to kill the seal and you do not want others to harm it, you must do something to chase it away. That's the only way to save its life."

"But what can I do, Big Lou? The seal is sticking to me like an icicle on my tongue."

"Then you must give him the cold shoulder."

"That won't be hard in this weather. It's forty degrees below," I said.

Mr. Hartz started playing the piano again. This time Michael sang "Give Him the Cold Shoulder."

"When your father says you can't take the
*   dogsled—not until you're older,*
Do what ev'ry smart Eskimo should do:
*   Give him the cold shoulder.*
When your little sister uses your muk-luks
*   no matter how many times you've told her,*
Do what ev'ry smart Eskimo should do:
*   Give her the cold shoulder.*
A nasty word will make your point,
*   like dropping a large heavy boulder.*

Sticks and stones may break their bones,
  but there's nothing like a cold shoulder.
So when your little seal comes back,
  and he's getting bolder,
You know what ev'ry smart Eskimo should do:
  Give him the cold shoulder."

The audience applauded again and Big Lou said, "What I'm telling you, Tuvat, is to duel with words. That is an old Eskimo tradition."

"Thanks, Big Lou. You've solved my problem."

So I left Big Lou and went out into the cold. And there was the little seal waiting for me.

"I don't want to hurt your feelings, but I don't want you to get killed," I said to Mickey. "Hey, fish breath, why don't you take a powder before I turn you into chowder? Why don't you give me a break before I turn you into steak? Why don't you scram before I turn you into ham!" Hearing my threats, the little seal put his head down and walked off sadly. "The cold shoulder really worked!" I said.

Well, after that I went over to my favorite hole in the ice and started fishing. But all of a sudden I slipped on the ice and I fell in the hole—right into the freezing water.

"Help!" I shouted. "Help me before I freeze!"

But there was no one around to help me—

until Mickey the seal came racing across the stage. He jumped in after me and pulled me to safety.

Afterward, I sat on the ice with the seal.

"Good work, Tuvat!" Josh Baldwin, my father, came back on stage with all the other villagers. "You've caught the seal. We'll have a feast tonight."

"Dad, have you gone snow-blind? This seal just saved my life!"

"Does that mean he won't be good with roasted potatoes?" Rejev said.

Just as they were about to grab the seal, I shouted, "Stop! Big Lou Igloo, help me!"

That was the signal for Big Lou to rush out and do something only Big Lou—well, really only Michael Thurman—could do. Michael came out and lifted Mickey Morgan over his head and held him there.

"Anyone who harms this seal will get the cold shoulder!" Big Lou shouted.

Then, after we all made friends with the seal, we all sang the last song in the show, "Iceberg Rock."

When the curtain came down, everyone in the audience was on their feet. Mr. Hartz kept playing the song as all of the actors lined up on the stage and took bows. We were so happy we were jumping up and down. Our parents were all swaying and clapping to the "Iceberg Rock."

Finally Mr. Hartz left the piano and came up on stage. "Ladies and gentlemen, moms and dads, I'd like you to meet the student who was one hundred percent responsible for tonight's play," he said, motioning for me with his finger.

"Here is our fifth-grade genius, Andrew Abel, our author and composer. Let's give him a special hand."

I'm not sure what happened next. It was as though I was watching myself from somewhere else. I walked across the stage listening to the audience cheer, and Mr. Hartz shook my hand and just wouldn't stop.

The next thing I knew, I was sitting in Dixon's and there was the Monster ice cream sundae sitting on the table in front of me. My mom and dad were sitting across from me, and we all had spoons in our hands.

"This is my son," my dad was telling the waiter and everyone else in the place. "We're celebrating. He wrote a play—a *musical* play. I've never laughed so hard in my life. He's going to be famous. There's no doubt in my mind."

I was almost getting embarrassed, so I changed the subject. "Hey, Dad, don't eat

all the hot fudge this time," I said with a smile.

"There's always more hot fudge," my father said, coming back down to earth. "You know, while we're on the subject, you'd better tell me again about this synthesizer keyboard you want."

The spoon fell out of my hand, splashed in the marshmallow syrup, and then dropped straight onto my lap. My dad rolled his eyes.

"You mean it, Dad?"

"Well, you're going to need it to write your class play next year, aren't you?"

"Right, Dad," I said.

"Besides," he said with a funny expression on his face. "The only reason I didn't buy it for you for Christmas was because I was afraid you'd let the lid fall on your fingers." Then he laughed to show it was a joke.

"Ha, ha, Dad," I said. "But the joke's on you: synthesizers don't have lids."

"They don't?" he said. "Good thing!" And this time we all laughed.